TILABEL

Patricia Coombs

EL DORADO

Lothrop, Lee & Shepard Company
A Division of William Morrow & Company, Inc.
New York

Other books by
PATRICIA COOMBS

Dorrie and the Amazing Magic Elixir
Dorrie and the Birthday Eggs
Dorrie and the Blue Witch
Dorrie and the Dreamyard Monsters
Dorrie and the Fortune Teller
Dorrie and the Goblin
Dorrie and the Halloween Plot
Dorrie and the Haunted House
Dorrie and the Weather-Box
Dorrie and the Witch Doctor
Dorrie and the Witch's Imp
Dorrie and the Wizard's Spell
Lisa and the Grompet
The Magic Pot
Molly Mullett
Mouse Café

Library of Congress Cataloging in Publication Data
Coombs, Patricia.   Tilabel.
SUMMARY: Inept Tilabel, forced to spin, weave, and sew for the groundhog
queen, is aided by three old "aunts," thus ensuring her marriage to the prince.
[1. Fairy tales.   2. Folklore—Germany]   I. Title.
PZ8.C7883Ti   813'.5'4 [398.2]   77-21039
ISBN 0-688-41831-7   ISBN 0-688-51831-1 lib. bdg.

First Edition
1   2   3   4   5   6   7   8   9   10

To my sister

Once upon a time, over a river, across a field, and down a hole, lived Tilabel. She lived with her hard-working mother.

Tilabel did not like to work. She liked to dance with her shadow in the field. When her mother sent her to pick grapes, Tilabel would swing on the vines. When her mother sent her to dig roots, Tilabel ran after butterflies.

One day Tilabel said, "Mother, the wild strawberries are ripe. Let's have a picnic."

"Picnic!" cried her mother. "It's time for you to learn to sew and spin. We have blankets and quilts to make before winter!"

"When I am Queen," said Tilabel dreamily, "we are going to have lots of holidays."

"Queen!" snapped her mother. "I'll crown you with a stick!" And she chased Tilabel down the hole. She sat her in front of the spinning wheel. She showed her how to spin.

"Get to work," said her mother. "I'm going to pile the roots for winter."

Tilabel began to spin. The wool caught in her paws. It made her sneeze. It got caught in her teeth. Her foot got stuck in the wheel. Her other foot got caught. She fell over.

Her mother was very angry. The next day she said to Tilabel, "Today you will learn to weave. Maybe you will do better at that than at spinning."

She sat Tilabel in front of the loom. She showed her how to weave.

"Get to work," said her mother. "I'm going to sort twigs for our winter beds."

Tilabel began to weave. It went badly. She wove the strings of her scarf in with the yarn. Her head got stuck in the loom.

Her mother grew angrier still. The next day she sat Tilabel down in a chair.

"You cannot spin. You cannot weave. You must learn to sew."

"But, Mother," said Tilabel, "the rain has stopped. The sun is shining. The birds are singing. The butterflies are flying. My shadow is stuck on the floor instead of dancing in the grass."

Her mother gave her a cuff on the ear. "SEW!" she said. She gave Tilabel needles and thread and pins. She gave her a basket of quilt squares to sew.

"Get busy," said her mother. "I'm staying right here to be sure you work."

Tilabel began to sew. It went badly. She stuck herself with pins and squealed. Her mother gave her a cuff. Tilabel howled.

While all this was going on down in the hole, the Queen came for a walk in the field. Hearing the squeals and howls and groans, the Queen stopped. She rapped on the roof of the hole.

Tilabel's mother stuck her head out. Her mouth dropped open.

"Your Majesty! This is a great honor!" she cried.

"Never mind that," said the Queen. "What's going on down there? I never heard such a racket!"

"Ah, oh, um," said Tilabel's mother. "It's only Tilabel. I wanted her to go out and play, but that girl thinks only of work. She spun all our wool in one day. Now she won't stop sewing for a minute."

"Really?" said the Queen with a smile. "She is just the person I need at the castle. Call her up here."

Tilabel came up out of the hole. She came very slowly. She had by mistake sewn the quilt to her lap, and her lap to the chair. Trying to gnaw through the thread, she had gotten it caught in her teeth. Needles and thread were hanging out of her mouth.

"Well, well," said the Queen, "I do like to see a person who sticks to her work. Come along with me, Tilabel. I can't get anyone to put in a good twelve hours work anymore."

"Oh, help," whispered Tilabel. She couldn't talk any louder because her mouth was full of needles and thread.

Tilabel's mother snipped off the chair. She snipped off the quilt. She snipped the threads from between Tilabel's teeth.

"Go with the Queen," said her mother. And off they went.

When they got to the castle, the Queen took Tilabel into the tower. There was a room with a spinning wheel and a loom. There were great sacks of wool.

A tear ran down Tilabel's cheek.

"There, there," said the Queen. "I know that seeing all that wool to be spun has made your heart overflow with joy. You can start to work right away. I'm sure you'll have it done by tomorrow. It will be Prince Grundel's birthday in a few days. We are having a big party. You will set him a good example. You can sit beside him and tell him the joys of work. He is, I fear, a dreamer."

With that, the Queen closed the door and locked it and was gone.

"Oh, woe is me!" cried Tilabel. She ran to the window. She tried to get out. The window was too small. She tried to chew through the door. It was too hard.

Tilabel stared at the spinning wheel. "I will try," she said, and she began to spin. The wool flew off the spindle. Then the yarn broke. The wool got caught in her paws. It got caught between her paws. At last she was all tangled up and couldn't get out.

It was getting dark. Tilabel was so tired. She closed her eyes. She wondered if she would ever see the sunlight and the field again.

All at once, she felt a tap on her shoulder. She opened one eye. She opened the other eye. There stood an old groundhog with teeth the color of buttercups. She looked so odd and so kind, Tilabel smiled. The old groundhog smiled back. She was all bent over, and one foot was as flat as a shovel.

"Don't cry, Tilabel," said the old groundhog. "I'll spin this wool for you. You have only to grant me one wish."

"Oh, gladly," said Tilabel. "With all my heart."

"Call me Aunt and ask me to Prince Grundel's birthday party," said the old groundhog.

"Dear Aunt," said Tilabel, "you will be there."

The old groundhog sat down at the spinning wheel and began to spin. The hum of the wheel was like the hum of bees, and Tilabel fell asleep.

When she woke up, the wool was all spun. The old Aunt had gone.

In came the Queen. She clapped her paws with joy when she saw that all the wool was spun. "You have done a good job," said the Queen. "Now you can weave the yarn into cloth and I will come back tomorrow."

The Queen was gone. Tilabel was alone. She stood and stared at the loom. She gave it a kick. "I would rather face a hungry wolf than this loom," she said.

Tilabel picked up the yarn. She sat down. She began to weave. She worked and worked at it. It went badly. It went worse. One paw got caught. Then the other paw got caught. She pulled. She tugged. She gave a great pull, and the loom fell over on top of her.

"Oh, help," said Tilabel. "I am done for. The Queen will boil me. Or pickle me. Or worse." She closed her eyes. A tear rolled down her cheek. The room grew dark.

All at once she felt a tap on her shoulder. Tilabel opened one eye. She opened the other. There stood an old, old groundhog. She looked so odd and so kind, Tilabel smiled through her tears. The old, old groundhog smiled back. She was all bent over, and one paw was as big as a frying pan.

"Don't cry, Tilabel," she said. "I will weave the yarn into cloth. You have only to grant me one wish."

"Oh, gladly," said Tilabel. "With all my heart."

"Call me Aunt and ask me to Prince Grundel's birthday party," said the old, old groundhog.

"Dear Aunt," said Tilabel, "you will be at the party."

The old, old groundhog sat down at the loom. She began to weave. Her paws flew to and fro. Tilabel fell fast asleep.

When Tilabel woke, the yarn was all spun into cloth. She rubbed her eyes. The old, old Aunt had gone.

In came the Queen. She chuckled when she saw all the yarn spun into cloth. She kissed Tilabel, and gave her a sewing basket.

"Well," said the Queen. "There is only one day left before Prince Grundel's birthday party. I am going to retire then and let him rule our Kingdom. I will come back tomorrow to get the shirts you have sewn for his birthday."

Then the Queen was gone and the door was locked. Tilabel was alone. She stared at the sewing basket. "I would rather it were a basket of snakes," said Tilabel. She took out the scissors. She took out the needles and thread. She took out the pattern and pins.

"Even with cuffs and whacks, my mother couldn't teach me to sew," sighed Tilabel. But she tried. She cut. She pinned. She pinned. She cut. By the time it grew dark, Tilabel had cut out only one shirt, and both sleeves were on the same side. She was very tired. Her eyes were red. Her paws hurt. Her back ached.

Tilabel began to cry. She put her head down on the shirt she had made. She sobbed.

All at once she felt a tap on her shoulder. She sniffed and opened her eyes. There stood an old, old, old groundhog. She looked so odd and so kind, Tilabel smiled. The old, old, old groundhog smiled back. She was all bent over. One of her eyes was shut in a squint. The other eye was big and red.

"Don't cry, Tilabel," she said. "I'll sew this cloth into shirts for you. You have only to grant me one wish."

"Oh, gladly," said Tilabel. "With all my heart."

"Very well," said the old, old, old groundhog. "Call me Aunt and ask me to Prince Grundel's birthday party."

"Dear Aunt," said Tilabel, "you will sit beside me."

The old, old, old groundhog bent over the cloth. Her big red eye blinked like a firefly as she cut and pinned and sewed. Tilabel fell fast asleep.

When Tilabel woke, all the cloth had been made into shirts. The old, old, old Aunt was gone.

In came the Queen. She laughed and clapped her paws when she saw the shirts all ready for the Prince.

"Dear Tilabel," said the Queen, "it will be hard for you to spend a day without working, but we must get ready for the party."

The Queen took Tilabel down into the castle. Tilabel was bathed and brushed. She had a nap on a big feather bed. Birds sang. Butterflies flew in and out. That night she was dressed in a fancy dress with beads and bows.

The Queen came and took Tilabel into the throne room. "Here are the shirts, all wrapped and tied, for you to give the Prince," said the Queen. "And here is Prince Grundel now."

Through the doors came the Prince. His boots were wet and muddy. He was carrying a fishing pole and a tangle of kite string.

The Queen stamped her foot and howled with rage. "Grundel! You have been off fooling around in the fields again!" cried the Queen. "You can't rule a kingdom wasting time like that!"

The Prince looked at Tilabel. Tilabel looked at the Prince. They both smiled.

"Hello," said the Prince, "I'm Grundel."

"Hello," said Tilabel, "I'm Tilabel. And here is a present for you. Happy Birthday!"

"I don't suppose they are kites," said the Prince. "Mine got stuck in a tree by the river."

"Never mind that," snorted the Queen. "The guests are here for the party."

Through the doors came the guests. The last to come in were the three old Aunts.

Tilabel laughed and ran to meet them. She hugged them and kissed them. She called them each Aunt, and brought them to meet the Prince.

Prince Grundel's mouth dropped open. "Excuse me," he said, "I do not mean to be rude. But it is a wonder to me that so pretty a groundhog as Tilabel has Aunts that look like you."

"Ah," said the first Aunt, "it is no wonder at all. Working day in and day out at the spinning wheel has bent my back. Working the treadle has made one foot as flat as a shovel."

"Ah," said the second Aunt, "it is no wonder at all. Working day in and day out at the loom has bent my back. Working the shuttle all day has made one paw as big as a frying pan."

"Ah," said the third Aunt, "it is no wonder at all. Snipping and sewing all day and by candlelight has shut one of my eyes in a squint and made my other eye big and red."

"Tilabel!" cried Prince Grundel. "You must never again touch a treadle or shuttle or needle. And since I am going to rule, I am going to order that no one work!"

"Not work!" cried the Queen, turning purple, then pale. "Not work! With you for a ruler the Kingdom is in for trouble. I am going to make Tilabel Queen!"

"All right," said Prince Grundel, "I will be Prime Minister."

"And Keeper of the Kites," said Tilabel.

"Long live Queen Tilabel!" shouted all the guests.

And Tilabel was a very good Queen. No one worked more than half a day, and Tilabel made up a lot of new holidays. Groundhog Day was everyone's favorite. If it was sunny that day, they ran back to bed for six more weeks of winter. If it was cloudy, they knew spring was near, and they danced in the meadow.